Quentin Blake

Mrs Armitage
and the
Big Wave

TED SMART

For Ali and Laurie and Lucy

MRS ARMITAGE AND THE BIG WAVE

This edition produced for The Book People Ltd,
Hall Wood Avenue, Haydock, St Helens, WA11 9UL

First published in Great Britain by Jonathan Cape,
an imprint of Random House Children's Books

Jonathan Cape edition published 1997
The Book People edition published 2006

1 3 5 7 9 10 8 6 4 2

Copyright © Quentin Blake, 1997

The right of Quentin Blake
to be identified as the author and illustrator of this work
has been asserted in accordance with the Copyright, Designs and Patents Act 1988.

RANDOM HOUSE CHILDREN'S BOOKS
61–63 Uxbridge Road, London W5 5SA
A division of The Random House Group Ltd

RANDOM HOUSE AUSTRALIA (PTY) LTD
20 Alfred Street, Milsons Point, Sydney,
New South Wales 2061, Australia

RANDOM HOUSE NEW ZEALAND LTD
18 Poland Road, Glenfield, Auckland 10, New Zealand

RANDOM HOUSE (PTY) LTD
Isle of Houghton, Corner Boundary Road & Carse O'Gowrie,
Houghton 2198, South Africa

RANDOM HOUSE INDIA PVT LTD
301 World Trade Tower, Hotel Intercontinental Grand Complex,
Barakhamba Lane, New Delhi 110001, India

THE RANDOM HOUSE GROUP Limited Reg. No. 954009

A CIP catalogue record for this book is available from the British Library.

Printed in China

Mrs Armitage was on her way to the beach.
She was wearing her surfing kit and she
carried her surfboard under her arm.
Breakspear the dog ran alongside.

When they got to the beach they walked
across the sand and into the water.

"What we have to do, Breakspear," said
Mrs Armitage, "is to swim out to sea
and wait for a Big Wave."

But while they were waiting for the
Big Wave Mrs Armitage could see
that Breakspear's little legs were getting tired.
"What we need here," said Mrs Armitage,
"is something to keep a faithful dog afloat."

So she swam back to the beach and bought
an inflatable desert island.

When she got back, Breakspear climbed
on to the desert island and they went
on waiting for the Big Wave.

But it was a hot, hot day and soon
Mrs Armitage was sweating and
Breakspear's tongue was hanging out.
"What we need here," said Mrs Armitage,
"is something to protect us from the sun's
powerful rays."

So she swam off and came back with
a cap with a yellow plastic brim for
herself and an umbrella with pink
spots for Breakspear; and they went
on waiting for the Big Wave.

Now they were nice and cool; but they soon began
to feel rather hungry, as you do at the seaside.
"What we need here," said Mrs Armitage,
"is a selection of light snacks to keep us going."

So she swam off and got a plastic duck and an
empty box and tied them together with string and
filled the box with tasty items.

When she got back Mrs Armitage ate an avocadoburger and Breakspear had some crunchy dog biscuits and they went on waiting for the Big Wave.

After a while a breeze sprang up and
blew briskly along the shore.
"This is delightful," said Mrs Armitage;
"but what we need here is something to
show us Wind Force and Direction."

And she swam off and came back with a wind stocking and a line of bunting and she fixed them so that they blew in the breeze, and Mrs Armitage and Breakspear went on waiting for the Big Wave.

A windsurfer passed them at high speed.
"Hi there, gorgeous!" he shouted.
"What we need here," said Mrs Armitage, "is
something we can hail fellow-sportsmen with."

And she swam off and came back
with a red megaphone. She brought
a motorhorn as well because it's always
a good thing to have a motorhorn.

Then she gave a few shouts and hoots and they went on waiting for the Big Wave.

By now all kinds of fish were popping
their heads out of the water to find
out what the fuss was about.
"I hope there aren't any sharks,"
said Mrs Armitage.
And she swam off...

…and came back with a sturdy boathook.
"Now we can give a prod to any sharks
that want to trouble us," said Mrs Armitage,
and they went on waiting for the Big Wave.

And then the Big Wave came.
At the same moment they noticed
a little girl called Miranda
who had swum out too far
and was in difficulties.

"Pah-hee-hah-hurgh," went Mrs Armitage
on the motorhorn. She hooked up Miranda
with the boathook and on they went.

They did a California slither,
a Bali swerve,
a Waikiki flip and ...

... arrived on the beach just in front
of Miranda's parents.

They all went to the beach café to celebrate.
"There's still time, Breakspear, for us to have
another go," said Mrs Armitage.

"But what we really need, what we *really* need, is…"